My Beloved

Shruti Dutta Gupta

Ukiyoto Publishing

All global publishing rights are held by

Ukiyoto Publishing

Published in 2023

Content Copyright © Shruti Dutta Gupta

ISBN 9789360169596

*All rights reserved.
No part of this publication may be reproduced,
transmitted, or stored in a retrieval system, in any form
by any means, electronic, mechanical, photocopying,
recording or otherwise, without the prior permission of
the publisher.*

The moral rights of the authors have been asserted.

*This is a work of fiction. Names, characters, businesses,
places, events, locales, and incidents are either the
products of the author's imagination or used in a fictitious
manner. Any resemblance to actual persons, living or
dead, or actual events is purely coincidental.*

*This book is sold subject to the condition that it shall not by
way of trade or otherwise, be lent, resold, hired out or
otherwise circulated, without the publisher's prior
consent, in any form of binding or cover other than that in
which it is published.*

www.ukiyoto.com

To the ten year old me who dreamt of being an author.

Contents

Chapter 1   1

Chapter 2   8

About the Author   13

Chapter 1

"Don't worry Chuni, we will get to the bottom of this," Premlata reassured her quivering daughter-in-law. "As long as you continue to stay inside and look after Sankar, no one would accuse you of anything,"

"But if I continue to stay inside, people would think that it didn't affect as much as it should," Chuni's tears continued to flow aimlessly and Premlata's efforts to make it stop seemed to be fruitless. "I will search for the culprit myself!" Chuni made a weak attempt to tie her long black as a raven's feather hair, "I won't rest until I find the culprit,"

Before Premlata could say anything Chuni had already gone outside the house. Without wasting any more of her time Premlata went to check on Sankar.

Sankar, the man of everyone's dreams! He had a face which was similar to actors, with his tall stature, big eyes, fair complexion and refined nose. Many relatives and villagers urged him to pursue an acting career but he couldn't bring himself to leave his beloved Chuni and act with some other woman. How could he? Chuni was the only one for him. No man was as bewitched with his wife as Sankar was with Chuni and to see such a wonderful man in this displeasing state was like a thorn that struck a chord in Premlata's tender heart.

"Babu, can you hear me?" Premlata asked in the softest tone a woman could bring herself to speak in. "Chuni will be here soon! Don't worry,"

"Please….Maa…save me!" Sankar mustered his strength as he spoke in his half-awake state. "She is going to kill me!" Sankar clutched his mother's white saree's hem.

"Who is going to kill you?" Premlata asked as she kept her palm on Sankar's forehead.

" O go, you are awake?" Chuni's honeyed voice made Premlata turn her head from her son to her daughter-in-law.

"Chuni come quick! Sankar is saying something,"

Chuni's weak attempt at tying her long hair was fruitless but that proved to be useful as she bent down to check on her beloved, her long strands of hair fell on her husband's face and calmed him down as he fell into a deep slumber.

"What happened, I thought you weren't going to rest until you found the culprit. See that's why I told you before, 'A woman's place is on her husband's feet', Premlata smirked. " Leave the hard stuff to the men!"

"You were right maa," Chuni brushed a lock of hair from her face and sat on the floor. "Did he tell you anything about what happened to him?" She slowly started to rub her beloved's foot with her hands.

"He was going, until you interrupted. Tell me, Chuni, Why weren't you with Sankar?" Premlata sat on the bed beside her son facing Chuni.

"I was asleep Maa, he went to get a glass of water by himself."

"See Chuni you are as irresponsible as ever! Why didn't you bring a jug of water in the first place? If you had done that my babu wouldn't be in this state now" Premlata heaved a deep sigh.

"Forgive me maa, I should have been careful" said Chuni as she wiped her tears.

"Who knows, maybe it was the work of a witch! Probably wanted my Sankar for herself,"

"Mine, you mean my Sankar," for a minute Chuni stopped crying and spoke in a sincere tone.

"Hush now Chuni! Don't take your husband's name!" Premlata widened her eyes as she fumed, for a minute she couldn't understand what escaped from the rose-tinted lips of her daughter-in-law "I knew you would only bring misfortune to my son!:

"Forgive me, maa," Chuni said, getting back to her meek voice.

"Chuni ma, Premlata!"

Both Chuni and Premlata turned their heads from each other and found Monojit babu standing at the doorway and beside him stood his daughter Saheli.

"Monojit babu, to whom do I owe this pleasure?" Premlata covered her head with the hem of her saree.

"I came as soon as I heard and I brought my daughter along for sweet Chuni," Monojit babu patted his daughter's head.

Sankar was supposed to marry Saheli however Premlata liked Chuni more for her son and ended up marrying him to Chuni. From there Premalata's family suffered a strained relationship with Monojit babu's family. However, this didn't stand in between a loving friendship between Monojit babu's daughter and Premlata's daughter-in-law.

"Chuni didi" Saheli made Chuni stand up on her feet " Let's get you inside, look at you, you are going to destroy your long beautiful hair if you don't tie it up, and let's wash your face,"

"Saheli!" Chuni said as she teared up. "My husband, everyone would think I did something to my beloved!"

"Chuni ma, don't worry my men are looking for the culprit, if it is the work of an outsider whoever it is will get caught, I promise you. No one would blame a sweet rose like you." Monoijit patted Chuni's head.

"Chuni go inside, don't make a scene!" Premlata ordered.

"Don't scold the poor child, Premlata. Chuni ma, go inside dear and try to get some sleep, whoever did that to poor Sankar would get punished, if not by men but by the gods", Monojit babu reassured Chuni as well as Premlata. However his reassuring efforts might have worked for the concerned mother, but the concerned wife was still drowning in the sea of turmoil.

"But what about those sinners, who don't get punished by men or the gods?" Chuni wiped her tears and looked towards Monojit babu who was speechless.

"Death won't be kind to them" Premlata put both of her hands on Chuni's shoulders, "Go inside Chuni, don't make me repeat myself",

"Forgive me Ma," Chuni covered her head with the hem of her red and white saree and turned to go inside with Saheli's help after giving one last look to her beloved.

After Chuni and Saheli were out of sight, Monojit babu went near Sankar and touched his sweaty forehead. "Poor boy, what happened to him?"

"Foolish Chuni! She let my Sankar out of her sight in the middle of the night. He got up to get a glass of water," Premlata lifted a glass from the tool that was beside Sankar's bed. "Chuni probably heard the sound of this glass falling and then she came here and discovered the result of her witless action,"

"Maybe something was in the water?"

"Who could tell, we have to wait for the doctor to get answers". Premlata heaved a brief sigh. " Do you think it was the work of a witch?"

"There is no such thing as a witch Premlata! I'm certain something was in the water, maybe some rat or cockroach got inside the earthen pot!"

Premlata and Monojit studied the room for a few seconds and discovered a large earthen pot in the corner of the room.

"How many times have I told Chuni to not put earthen pots in the corner? Who knows what got inside? Premlata and Monojit babu removed the cloth cover from the pot only to find it empty and dry as a bone.

"It is hard to poison an earthen pot if there is nothing inside, do you have any other pots from where Sankar might have got the water, perhaps from a jug?"

"I don't know. Let's ask foolish Chuni!"

"Premlata it's your house as well, why are you placing all the blame on her?"

"Monojit babu please, as much as I appreciate your concern it is not your place to advise me on how to run my household,"

"It might have been,"

"Yes, it might have been," Premlata smirked.

"But I am glad it is not," now it was Monojit babu's turn to smirk.

Chapter 2

Saheli took Chuni inside and made her sit in front of the mirror. "Look at you, Chuni didi, what have you done to yourself?", Saheli started to wipe sweat on Chuni's face with a white cloth which was lying on Chuni and Sankar's bed. "Sankar dada is going to be fine, there is no force in this world that can keep him away from you,"

"You think so?" Chuni took her hairbrush and slowly started to brush her hair.

"I know so Chuni didi," Saheli let out a chuckle and sat on the bed. "I still remember the day when Sankar dada wouldn't let you stay over for one night at our place, he was this close to dragging you from me. To have a husband who can't stay away for one night is a dream for many women, how did you bewitch him, did you put a love spell on him?"

" Only witches cast spells, are you by any chance calling me a witch my dear Saheli?" Chuni stopped brushing her hair and turned her face from the mirror to her friend.

"God no, I have never seen a witch this kind," Saheli giggled.

"You have never seen a witch," Chuni turned her face back to the mirror as she cracked a small smile.

"Let me help you with that Chuni didi," Saheli grabbed the hair brush from her friend's hand and started brushing her hair. "You have such long beautiful hair", she squealed.

"My beloved likes my hair so much, he always tells me to wear my hair down,"

"Who wouldn't? Even I too like your hair,"

"Do you like my hair more than me?" Chuni who was looking down finally looked up and met her friend's gaze in the mirror. "Would you like me less if I was bald?"

"Don't be silly Chuni didi," Saheli pinched both of Chuni's cheeks and planted a kiss on her forehead. "Just like there is no force that could keep Sankar dada away from you, there is no force in this world that could make me love you any less,"

Chuni smiled and opened her mouth to say something but got interrupted by Premlata.

"Chuni! Premlata rushed in like a storm. A storm that could gobble down everyone that will come in its way.

"Yes maa," Chuni stood up from her seat and covered her head with the hem of her saree.

"Tell me where did you store the rest of the water, because I checked the kitchen and there was no sign of any matka, unless you were planning to kill me and my babu out of dehydration then I would like an explanation!"

Chuni pointed her forefinger towards a jug that was on the bedside table, Premlata followed her gaze, picked up the jug and found water inside it.

"This must have been the water that Sankar drank," Premlata observed the water inside the jug as if watching it closely would allow the poison to jump up from the water and vanish in thin air.

"What is going on?" Saheli asked,

"Your father thinks that Sankar might have been poisoned, here Chuni, why don't you drink it to prove that Monojit babu is wrong," Premlata offered the jug to her daughter-in-law.

"What are you saying? If my father is correct then Chuni didi might share the same fate as Sankar dada, you can't put her life at risk!" Saheli cried out.

"Why not? She put my son's life at risk! It is only fair that she compensates for it with her own life, and what's more honorable for a woman than sharing the same fate as her husband?" Premlata cracked out a small smile. "Don't make me repeat myself, Chuni,"

"Please don't make her do this," Saheli uttered in a weak voice, it was like watching a pack of wolves devour her friend, she knew her friend couldn't run away as her feet were stuck in the ground, the only way to save her was to convince the wolves.

"I'll do anything for my beloved," Chuni finally spoke up and took the jug from her mother-in-law. It looks like Saheli couldn't convince the wolves at last.

Both Premlata and Saheli watched Chuni in anticipation as she gulped down the whole jug of water. Both of them expected Chuni to hit the ground, however, she stood still as the stump of a tree.

"Maybe the gods are not ready to give me the honor of sharing the same fate as my beloved, what should I do maa?" Chuni spoke as she again started sobbing.

"Shut your mouth, Chuni! people have started to visit, come out so people don't suspect you to be the one behind your husband's condition" Premlata grabbed the jug from her daughter-in-law and stormed outside.

"No one would suspect you Chuni didi, everyone in the village knows how much of a devoted wife you are," Saheli consoled her friend. "Although I still need to brush your hair,"

My beloved

Chuni again sat on the tool in front of the mirror and let her friend brush her hair. As Saheli was brushing her hair she noticed red scars on Chuni's back, the type of scars that slaves had on their backs. Saheli touched those scars and earned a wince from her friend.

"Chuni didi, what is all this?" Saheli frowned.

"A sign of love from my beloved," said Chuni.

"Chuni didi, did Sankar dada do this to you?" Saheli herself couldn't believe what just escaped from her mouth.

However, Chuni kept quiet and tied her hair in a loose bun to give her friend a better look at her back.

"Chuni!" Premlata's alarming voice made Chuni and Saheli rush outside on the veranda only to find her crying over her son's body along with other villagers. Saheli noticed that Sankar's lips had turned purple.

"And that is a sign of love from me to my beloved," Chuni whispered into Saheli's ear and joined her mother-in-law after wearing her hair down and covering her head with the hem of her saree.

About the Author

Shruti Dutta Gupta is a passionate writer who has been captivated by the realms of horror, fantasy, and mystery from an early age. Her journey as a writer began in the margins of school notebooks, where she would weave chilling tales that left her classmates both spellbound and spooked. With an innate love for storytelling, she ventured into the world of writing, focusing on her two greatest literary passions—horror and mystery. When Shruti isn't busy crafting tales of the supernatural and the mysterious, she can often be found delving into the works of other authors in the same genres, drawing inspiration from the masters of horror and mystery. With each word she writes, Shruti aspires to leave her readers with a sense of wonder and an insatiable craving for the unknown.

Stay tuned for more spine-tingling stories from this emerging author, as she continues to explore the depths of the human psyche through her passion for horror and mystery.